First published in paperback in Great Britain by HarperCollins Children's Books in 2006

1 3 5 7 9 10 8 6 4 2

ISBN-13: 978-0-00-718241-1

ISBN-10: 0-00-718241-4

Text and illustrations copyright © Emma Chichester Clark 2006

HarperCollins Children's Books is a division of HarperCollins Publishers Ltd.

The author/illustrator asserts the moral right to be identified as the author/illustrator of the work.

A CIP catalogue record for this title is available from the British Library.

Visit our website at: www.harpercollinschildrensbooks.co.uk

Printed and bound in Singapore

Melrose and Croc

FIND A SMILE

by Emma Chichester Clark

HarperCollins *Children's Books*

It was a lovely sunny day,
but something was wrong.
"What's happened?"
asked Little Green Croc.

"I've lost my smile," said Melrose.

"Well, let's go and find it then!" said Little Green Croc.

Melrose and Little Green Croc got in the car
and drove out to the country.

"But how will we find it?" asked Melrose.

"Well," said Little Green Croc,

"first, we have to run, as fast as we can...

...just like this!"

"Then we have to hop over a stream,
without touching the water...

...just like this!" said Little Green Croc.

"Then we have to chase a squirrel up a tree,

just like this…

...and say hello to every cow,

just like this!" said Little Green Croc.

"Next, we find a yellow flower and smell it,"
said Little Green Croc, "just like this…

and catch a falling leaf, just like this…

...which you wear on your nose, just like this,

and walk backwards up the hill, just like this!"
said Little Green Croc.

"Then you sit in a special place and forget about everything," said Little Green Croc.

"What were we looking for?"
asked Little Green Croc.

"I can't remember!" said Melrose,
and he smiled, just like this!

Read about how Melrose and Croc first met…

Melrose and Croc

by Emma Chichester Clark

Hardback ISBN: 0-00-719729-2

It is Christmas Eve, and both Melrose and Croc are all alone in the city.
They dream of a wonderful Christmas but feel sad for they have no one
to share it with. And so it might have been were it not for the sound of
beautiful music and a chance encounter. Could this be the beginning of
a happy Christmas and even the start of a wonderful friendship?

...and how they became the best of friends.

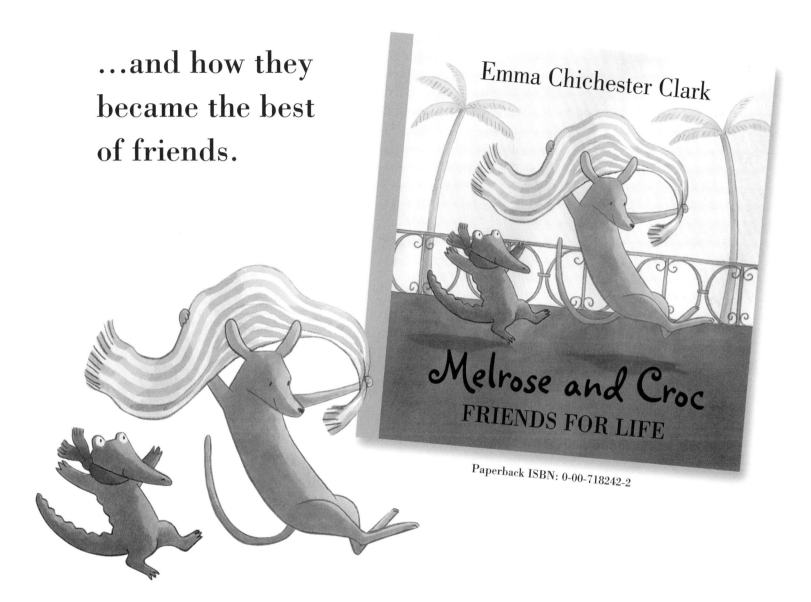

Emma Chichester Clark

Melrose and Croc
FRIENDS FOR LIFE

Paperback ISBN: 0-00-718242-2

Melrose and Croc love all kinds of things about each other, like being able to do somersaults or draw aeroplanes. Sometimes Croc wishes he were more like Melrose... until his friend reminds him that being different is what makes him extra special.

Look out for other new titles about Melrose and Croc, coming soon!